TWISTED
FAIRY TALES

The Three Little NARWHALS

Stewart Ross

Capella

This edition published in 2019 by Arcturus Publishing Limited
26/27 Bickels Yard, 151–153 Bermondsey Street,
London SE1 3HA

Written by: Stewart Ross
Illustrated by: Chris Jevons
Designed by: Jeni Child
Edited by: Sebastian Rydberg

ISBN: 978-1-83857-048-4
CH007845NT
Supplier 33, Date 0819, Print run 9224

Printed in China

Once, on the cold green sea, there sailed a pirate ship belonging to some very greedy pirates. The crew was so busy counting their treasure that they didn't notice a great storm coming.

Huge waves picked up their ship, spun it around, and smashed it back into the sea. The pirates swam to a rocky island, but their ship sank like a stone.

Deep down below the surface of the stormy sea swam three little narwhal siblings.

"Jumping jellyfish!" they cried as the pirate ship came bubbling down beside them. "Let's go take a look!"

Spike, the eldest of the narwhal family, had a pointy horn that he used to open oysters. His sister, Spiral, had a twisty horn. It would have been good as a corkscrew, but she didn't have any bottles with corks in the tops. Stubby, the youngest, hardly had a horn at all—he just had a little bump.

All three watched in amazement as the pirate ship settled on the sandy ocean floor.

"Aha!" said Spike. "I know what it is!"

"Well, what is it?" asked Spiral.

"It's a ship!" exclaimed Spike.

Spiral frowned. "But what's it *for?*"

Spike wiggled his horn in an important manner and replied, "It's for... Well, it's for ... Sort of... Er—"

“I know what it’s for,” interrupted Stubby. “It’s for making things.”

“Ooo! What sort of things?” said Spiral excitedly.

Stubby thought for a moment. “Well, anything you want. Especially houses.”

So each little narwhal started to build a house from parts of the pirate ship.

"I'm the oldest *and* the fastest swimmer," boasted Spike, "so I have first choice."

He zoomed up to the ship and began collecting the top parts. He took ropes and sails, poles, and masts. Humming to himself, he propped them up on the ocean floor and made a sort of makeshift tent.

When the tent was finished, he swam back to admire it. His chest swelled with pride. "Though I say it myself, that's *some* house!" he crowed.

At that very moment, a family of dolphins came swimming by. "Hey, guys," called Spike, "what do you think of this, huh?"

"Think of what?" asked the mother dolphin, trying to keep a straight face.

"My fan-tas-tic new crib." said Spike. They looked at him blankly. "Crib," he explained, "is a cool word for house."

"Ah! So that's what it is," replied the mother dolphin. "It's, er, beautiful!"

Her children were not so polite. "*House*, Mama?" They giggled. "It looks more like a squished jellyfish!"

Still giggling, the dolphin family swam off to look at the other narwhal houses.

After the dolphins had gone, Spike went inside to check out his new house.

"Wow!" he said to himself. "This place is so-o-o awesome!"

To let everyone nearby know how well he'd done, he sang a boasting song: "My house is best! Better than the rest!"

As Spike was singing, the big, bad shark came cruising by. The food he loved more than any other was lovely, juicy whale. But he hadn't seen one for days, and he was very hungry. Seeing Spike's new house, he stopped and listened.

Well, well, well, he thought. *Or should I say: whale, whale, whale! A singing meal!*

The big, bad shark swam around the

house, looking for a way in. *The doors and windows are too small,* he thought. *But those walls don't look very strong.*

He opened his enormous jaws with teeth as sharp as swords and shouted, "I'll crunch and I'll munch and I'll have this house for lunch!"

What he really wanted to eat, of course, was not the house but the little narwhal inside!

When Spike heard the big, bad shark was planning to have his house for lunch, he wondered whether his home was quite as cool as he'd thought.

Crunch! Munch! went the shark's jaws on the sails and ropes. Spike stared at the teeth as sharp as swords—and decided his house wasn't cool at all!

"Time to move, Spikey!" he said to himself. "Goodbye, awesome house!"

Luckily, narwhals are much better at swimming than house-building. As the big, bad shark mashed up the front of his house, Spike dashed out the back door. With the flick of a fin, he swam around to his sister's house.

"Hi, Spiral!" he cried. "I've come for a sleepover, okay?"

"Sure, brother," said Spiral. "But what's wrong with your house?"

"It kind of got of munched!"

"Munched?" Spiral gasped.

"Yeah. The big, bad shark decided to have it for lunch. He wanted to have me as a side dish, but I was wa-a-ay too fast for him!"

Spiral had built her house with wood from the pirate ship. She had decorated it with coral, seaweed, and shells. As she showed Spike around, she explained how beautiful it was, in case he couldn't tell.

"Look at the shiny shells, Spikey!" she exclaimed. "Aren't they so chic?"

"And the seaweed on the roof even glows in the dark," she went on. "All my friends will be so jealous!"

Spike nodded. Yes, it really was an attractive house. But he was a little sad, because he no longer had one himself.

"It looks great, Spiral," he said. "And your door's way sturdier than mine was!"

"I sure hope it's shark-proof!" cried Spiral. "I don't want that big, bad meanie chewing up my beautiful house—with us inside it!"

Nearby, the dolphin family was admiring Spiral's work. "It's a lovely house, Mother," said the youngest dolphin, who always told the truth. "But won't the shark see it from far away?"

"Maybe," replied her mother. "We'll soon find out."

The big, bad shark hadn't noticed Spike leaving by his back door. So when he had finished crunching and munching and found no narwhal inside, he was very angry. He was hungrier than ever too.

Where's that little whale-thing gone? he wondered.

Peering around the ocean floor, he spotted something pink and glowing. It was the shiny coral on Spiral's roof!

Aha! he thought. *What have we here?*

He cruised up to the pretty house and listened. Spike was happy now that he had helped his sister decorate her door, and the two narwhals were singing together proudly: "Our house is best! Better than the rest!"

Whale, whale, whale, thought the shark. *Another singing meal! Two dishes this time.*

He searched for a way in. Finding the door and windows too small, he opened his enormous jaws with teeth as sharp as swords and shouted, "I'll crunch and I'll munch and I'll have this house for lunch!"

What he meant, of course, was not the house but the two little narwhals inside!

"Oh my!" exclaimed Spiral when she heard the shark outside. "What's that?"

"I know what it is!" wailed Spike. "It's the big, bad shark with teeth as sharp as swords. And it's his munch-time!"

As Spike spoke, the shark started to eat his way into the house. *Snap!* went the enormous jaws. *Chomp! Chomp! Snap!* He bit through the wooden walls, he chewed up the "shark-proof" door, and he chomped away the roof decorated with green seaweed.

"My beautiful house!" wailed Spiral.

"Forget your house!" cried Spike. "It's your tail you need to save. Let's go!"

With a flick of a fin, the little narwhals zipped out through the back door and swam around to Stubby's house.

"Hi, Stubbs," Spiral said, panting. "We've come for a sleepover, okay?"

"Of course." He smiled shyly. "But what's wrong with your houses?"

Spike and Spiral looked embarrassed. "We sort of ran into a munching shark," explained Spike.

"He wanted to eat us!" continued Spiral. "But we were way too speedy for him."

"Glad you got away!" said Stubby. "Welcome to my house. You can stay here as long as you want."

"Thanks a lot," chorused Spike and Spiral. "We don't like being out in the open with the big, bad shark sneaking around."

Spike stared at Stubby's house. "Nice place you've built here, Stubbs," he said with a grin. "But, excuse me, it looks a little weird."

"It's not exactly beautiful, is it? It could do with more windows." added Spiral.

Stubby shook his head. "You're right. It is a little weird and ugly and dark, but it's the best I could do."

He explained that he couldn't use ropes and sails from the pirate ship because Spike had taken them for his house. He couldn't use wood, either, because Spiral had taken it for hers.

The two older narwhals had left only the metal pieces of the pirate ship. And that's what Stubby had used.

"Metal?" exclaimed Spike.

"Yes," Stubby went on. "I had to build my house out of cannons, chains, and cutlasses."

"Cannons, chains, and cutlasses!" exclaimed Spike. "No wonder your house looks weird, Stubbs!"

"Looks aren't everything," he replied quietly.

"You're right," said Spiral kindly. "And it looks strong enough to keep out munching, crunching sharks."

When he looked around, Spike agreed, and soon the three little narwhals were

singing together loudly in Stubby's weird but wonderful house.

"This house may not be sparkly," sang Spiral.

"It may not be great for parties," continued Spike.

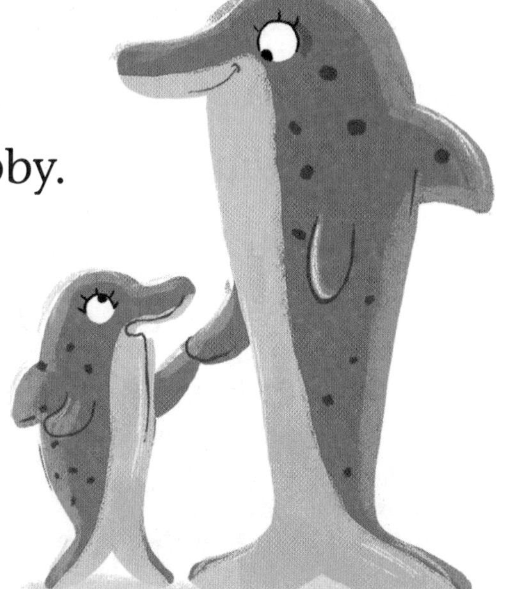

"But we'll stay here in the dark, see?" sang Stubby.

"While we're hiding from the shark-y!" they all chorused together.

Not far away, the dolphin family was also looking at Stubby's house. Like Spike, they thought it was really odd.

"In fact," said the youngest dolphin, "it's the craziest house I've ever seen."

"Maybe," said her mother, "but looks aren't everything." She glanced around anxiously. "Even so, I wish they wouldn't sing. I'm afraid the Big Bad You-Know-Who will hear them."

The big, bad shark was now very, very hungry. He had seen two juicy whale-things, which had made his mouth water, but he hadn't managed to catch them.

Hearing the three little narwhals singing in Stubby's house, he thought, *Whale, whale, whale... Yet another singing meal! And this time there are three dishes: an appetizer, a main course, and a dessert!*

Once again, he swam around the house, looking for a way in. Finding the door and windows too small, he opened his enormous jaws with teeth as sharp as swords. Then he began, "I'll crunch and I'll munch—"

But someone else said, "And I'll have this house for lunch!"

Hey! thought the shark. *Who dares use my special dinner-time poem?*

It was the three little narwhals! Spike and Spiral had heard the rhyme before and had taught it to Stubby. They couldn't stop giggling.

The big, bad shark was absolutely furious. "Right!" he bellowed. "ATTA-A-ACK!"

Hearing a swishing noise, Spiral glanced out the window—and stopped giggling. "Oh no!" she wailed. "He's seen us!"

Spike and Stubby joined their sister and looked outside. The big, bad shark was heading straight toward them like a torpedo. His jaws were open, his eyes gleamed with anger, and now his teeth looked more like spears than swords.

Spike suddenly remembered something. "It's all right, everybody. Don't panic!" he called. "This house is made of cannons, remember? Stubbs, get them ready!"

The shark was so close, they could see pieces of seaweed stuck in his teeth.

"That won't work!" wailed Stubby. "We have to strike a match to fire the cannons—and matches won't light underwater! Look out!"

As Stubby finished speaking, the shark reached the house and closed his jaws with a tremendous *SNAP!*

The youngest dolphin, watching from a safe distance, covered her eyes with her fins. "I can't watch!" she cried. "It's too terrible! Poor little narwhals!"

The big, bad shark was very good at things that didn't need brainpower, like eating. But he was not very good at *thinking* or *noticing*.

He said the same rhyme over and over again because he couldn't *think* of anything else. And he hadn't *noticed* Spike and Spiral escaping out the back doors of their houses. He hadn't noticed ships sailing on the sea above him either. And he certainly hadn't noticed the pirate ship made of rope and sails and wood—and metal.

In fact, he didn't know what metal was. That was his problem—his really big problem.

As Stubby cried, "Look out!" and the youngest dolphin covered her eyes and sobbed, the angry shark closed its enormous jaws over a large brass cannon.

There was a clinky, crashy, crunchy noise as his teeth as sharp as swords bit on the big brass gun.

A second later he let out a long and furious howl. "OOOWWWWWWWWWWWW!"

At first no one spoke. Eventually Stubby put his head out the window and said with a smile, "Mr. Shark, I believe cannons are made for shooting, not eating."

The big, bad shark glared at him but said nothing.

Spike popped up beside Stubby and added with a grin, "He's right, you know, Sharky. You can't crunch cannons."

Still the big, bad shark said nothing.

"And even if you did manage," said Spiral, trying not to giggle, "they would give you a terrible tummy ache!"

The big, bad shark had heard enough. But when he opened his jaw to reply, the three little narwhals fell over laughing. His jaw was empty! When he'd bitten the big brass cannon, he'd knocked all his teeth out. There they were, scattered across the ocean floor. He champed his pink gums together in fury.

"Beh whyert!" he commanded. He meant to say, "Be quiet!" but speaking without teeth makes the words sound different.

Even the dolphins started laughing.

With everyone watching, the shark picked up his teeth from the sandy bottom and swam away. As he left, he said, “Ahm hoeing hoo bind eh tempest hoo foot hem baa,” which meant, “I’m going to find a dentist to put them back.”

“Hen hile hum baa (Then I’ll come back),” he warned, “hand heat ewe haul hup! (and eat you all up!)" Whether or not he found a dentist, we will never know, because no one ever saw him again.

The dolphin family swam over to tell the three little narwhals how brave they were. Could they do anything to help? they asked.

"Yes, please," replied Stubby. "My house is too small for all three of us. We need to make it bigger."

"Can we help?" said the little dolphin to his mother.

"Of course we can," she said. "There are plenty of pieces of rope and sail and wood where Spike's and Spiral's houses used to be. Let's use them to build you a bigger and better house, Stubby."

The narwhals and dolphins built a fine new home. When it was finished, they wrote NARWHAL MANSION on a board beside the front door. Underneath they wrote SHARKS KEEP OUT.

The story of how the three little narwhals defeated the big, bad shark spread throughout the ocean. Fish of every kind came to meet the three heroes and see their famous mansion.

Well, not fish of every kind. They never once got a visit from a shark.